Her Dangerous Passion

Anastasia's journey to becoming a hotwife

TJ Mack

Dedicated to all those who have inspired

Contents

Title Page

Copyright

Dedication

Introduction

Prologue

Chapter One   1

Chapter Two   3

Chapter Three   10

Chapter Four   19

Chapter Five   24

Chapter Six   32

About The Author   35

Introduction

This is the first book of a new series.
If you enjoy reading it please leave a review!

Prologue

"This man would not kiss me as I like to be kissed but as he does. His way is too hard, demanding,dangerous. His way is not love. It is passion and it burns. Incinerates."

Karen Marie Moning

Chapter One

"**S**orry darling, I've been feeling tired recently. I will try better next time." Timothy pulled back the bedsheets and turned away with his head in the pillow. It was the third night in a row he had failed to maintain an erection. Anastasia, his beautiful wife turned away trying hard not to show her disappointment, indeed at this stage frustration.

"Ok Timothy," she mumbled. "Good night I guess." She closed her eyes in frustration. It was the same last weekend too. She knew he had been working hard in his job at the office call centre and his boss had been giving him a hard time for underperforming results. But now he was underperforming in the bedroom as well.

Anastasia knew from when they met 2 years ago that Timothy was no Lothario bedroom stud, but he had at least been able to perform adequately once a week at weekends. But recently even that was proving too much for him. She had questioned herself and if she was still attractive to him. With her golden blonde shoulder length hair and innocent but potentially naughty blue eyes, she knew she was attractive to men. Her slim 5'9 tall figure was complimented by great long legs, which she used to strut confidently on the runway when she did modelling at fashion shows while a student. She was often told she looked like the Victoria's Secret model Candice Swanepoel, which was a great compliment. In her job as an air hostess, she was always the subject of male attention from the passengers. The prying eyes and the lewd comments. As a professional she could handle it of course. She had to admit that some of it she quite enjoyed, especially if it was from a charming, handsome passenger in business class.

She had never taken up any of the numerous opportunities and offers she received. After all, Timothy was a loyal and sweet boyfriend. Deep down she knew that she could have any man she wanted and sex with a long list of willing potential partners. But wild sexual pleasure was perhaps missing from her relationship. No, not perhaps it definitely was she thought.

And after 2 years with Timothy that was not likely to change. These thoughts swirled around in her head as she tried to get to sleep, only interrupted by the sound of his snoring. Surely there was more to a relationship than mind blowing, exhilarating and life changing sex? Wasn't there? Was there?? Maybe there was not.

Anastasia remembered a conversation she and Timothy had recently after another occasion when he had failed to get an erection in bed. He had suggested that maybe she could see other people if she wanted to, and "have fun". "Anastasia, it would excite me if you were with another man," he had told her. She had been shocked that he had suggested such a thing and had dismissed it as something said when over emotional, telling him that it was something "other people do" and "only happened in porn films". But now Timothy's inadequacies had begun to frustrate her and she maybe had to consider the possibility.

She did not want to leave him but she knew she deserved great sex. She deserved better than what she was getting right now. Deep down she had the uncomfortable feeling that she could do better than Timothy. Why couldn't he get a better job than this one that tired him out and paid only £20,000 a year she had constantly asked him, but with no action from him. Why couldn't he go to the gym and get fit she had suggested several times, but to no avail. Maybe it was time for her to take up his suggestion and give herself what she deserved.

Chapter Two

The flight from New York JFK to London Heathrow was so far a routine flight for Anastasia. She knew she looked stunning in her red Virgin Atlantic uniform. Serving the business class passengers was generally more pleasurable with a more polite clientele. She had served the drinks and was about to take her scheduled break when she heard a deep voice from behind the corner of her ear.

"Excuse me mam, but I have no ice". She looked around faster than she normally would in response to this regular type of passenger request. "I always have ice with my scotch".

The deep voice turned into a half smile. The American accent belonged to a rather distinguished looking gentleman in seat 39F. "I do apologize sir; I will get some for you". Anastasia took some ice from the bucket on her trolley and placed it in his glass.

"Thank you, mam," he smiled at her, as she smiled at him longer than the normal polite customer service etiquette would require.

She noticed the glint in his blue eyes, which she thought complimented his blond hair and light sun kissed skin. His tan was just the right shade of golden. Probably she assumed from a weekend at the Hamptons or in Florida like a lot of passengers on business class. "You seem busy tonight," he enquired.
"Yes, this flight is usually busy, thankfully getting back to normal after covid. That's how we like it". She had now turned round to give the handsome American her full attention.

He smiled again, this time making eye contact with her for a couple of seconds longer. She noticed again the deepness of his blue eyes and whiteness of his teeth, just right for a man in his mid 30s who clearly looked after himself. The Wall Street Journal and Financial Times laid on his table beside his Apple laptop and Armani suit jacket. She had always loved the design on a man, but Timothy never wore a suit. He had no reason to. She wished he had.

"We will be landing in about an hour I guess," he enquired as he checked his watch. A Rolex naturally.

He was clearly a man with impeccable taste.

"'Yes, around 9pm London time" she happily informed him. "Still enough time to enjoy the night".

Anastasia wasn't sure why she had said the last sentence with a mischievous smile when a polite guidance of the landing time would have been sufficient.

"I always make the time to enjoy the night," he responded with equal mischievousness. "I hope the traffic in Knightsbridge is less busy this time of night for me. My London apartment is there."

He leaned back on his seat, arms behind head. "So, I should be just fine," smiling again at Anastasia. "You live in London?" she excitedly asked.

"I live in both London and New York. Don't know how you Brits can cope with the winter cold. In summer I have to go to Cali and get my surfing in." His deep voice was becoming more attractive by the minute.

"Somehow we cope," she laughed.

This was how he got his natural tan she thought. He did have that surfer look of blond hair and blue eyes, alongside a chiselled manly jawline. It was a look on a man which always held an attraction to her. Her first serious boyfriend was similar and had also been a surfer on the South coast of London during the summer. Anastasia was glad she had afforded the time to talk to this charming and indeed very handsome man.

"My surfing sure helps to relax from business. And we all need fun sometimes, don't we? "It was the way he said it slowly and intently at Anastasia that almost made her blush. Not quite red faced, but her face now had a bit of a glow.

She was used to men from business class trying it on with her, as was to be expected with a beautiful, blonde leggy air hostess. But they were mostly boring, sleazy and unattractive. Most men would be too intimidated to approach her as they would consider her out of their league.

But this handsome passenger had the confidence to do it and in a classy manner. "Oh yes we certainly do," she replied, finding herself flustered and hot. So much so that the next second she knocked one of the forks on the table onto the floor.

"Oh gosh I am sorry!" she quickly apologized as she knelt down to pick it up. A glimpse of her stocking tops became visible as the skirt hitched up which he could not fail to notice.

"Allow me," he interjected, getting up from his seat and handing it slowly back to Anastasia. His large strong hand brushing up against her hand as he did so.

"Thank you," she smiled. As he stood up Anastasia noticed the full length of his body and physique. He was around 6'2 tall with broad shoulders filling out his blue shirt.

"Anytime. My pleasure".

That smile of his again caught Anastasia lowering her gaze in gentle embarrassment. Was it that obvious that she was so flustered? And that he was the reason?

"I better get back," Anastasia said, knowing that she had stayed for longer than was considered professional.

"Yes, your colleagues will wonder where you are," he told her.

She quickly and excitedly made her way back down the aisle hoping that her interaction with the hunk in seat 39F had not been noticed. No such luck. Her flight attendant colleagues Lucy and Jessica had been watching it all.

"Omg Anna, who is he??" Lucy excitedly asked as she returned.

"He is gorgeous!" said Jessica, trying not to be heard by the passengers.

"Well, he is American, a businessman with an apartment in Knightsbridge". Anastasia was hoping it had not raised eyebrows but was equally excited to be telling someone.

"Wow, he is so perfect Anna!" Jessica could barely contain herself. "I tried to get his attention earlier," she said, "but he was reading his Wall Street Journal. Damn!" They were all giggling like schoolgirls in the corner rather than flight attendants at 30,000 feet above the Atlantic.

"Yes, he is rather hot," Anastasia coyly admitted to them.

She surprised herself that she had just openly said this. It would have been the first time she had ever openly admitted to the attractiveness of another man since she was with Timothy. She did feel a tinge of guilt but what was wrong with a bit of harmless flirting?

"I think he likes you Anna," said Lucy. "I saw the way he looked at you".

"Oh, he was just being polite I'm sure," was her not entirely convincing response. "Do you think he really does? "Anastasia was trying not to sound too excited or interested in the answer.

"Definitely. Imagine being with a man like that. What a dreamboat!" Jessica wistfully pronounced. "Yes, it would be quite something," Anastasia murmured as she went silent for a moment, seemingly contemplating such a prospect. They then all broke out in giggles again as they peered down the aisle hoping to catch a glimpse of the Adonis in seat 39F.

Anastasia decided that before the flight landed, she would make sure she checked with him again just to make sure he had enjoyed the flight and to thank him for picking up the dropped cutlery. It was just the polite thing to do and so what if she would never normally do this with a customer, it was good customer service right?

But she felt her heart beating a little faster as she walked down the aisle towards him, checking her lipstick and make up were still all good. A smile broke out between them as he noticed her approaching him. "Hello again Sir, I hope everything on the flight this evening was to your satisfaction?" He grinned satisfyingly.

"Oh yes definitely. Your service was excellent. I'm Brad, nice to meet you". Offering her his hand, she held it slowly in response, feeling how large and manly his hand was.

"I'm Anastasia," she replied.

This time the gaze between them was even more intense, as he kissed her hand gently, making her heart beat so much faster she could almost hear it.

"Anastasia, let me take you out in London. I know a place in Piccadilly that is fantastic. Great food. You would love it." She was both taken aback and excited simultaneously by his forwardness. Who was she trying to fool? She had wanted him to take the initiative.

"Well, I'm flattered. I am busy the next few days," she responded trying not to sound too keen or over excited. "But maybe I am free on..."

"I will take you out this Saturday evening," he interjected with such confidence. "Give me your number," he asked as he took out his phone and switched it on. Anastasia knew that she was supposed to tell passengers that no phone or electronics could be switched on before landing, but she was now too flustered to tell him. She sheepishly looked around the cabin hoping none of the passengers or fellow crew had seen. Not to mention of course the fact that she was about to give her number to a passenger, which was against company guidelines.

Naturally he had the latest new iPhone edition, one which Timothy had wanted to buy but could not due to the hefty price tag. Anastasia quickly gave him her number as he entered it into his contacts list, which she noticed was a long list as he scrolled down.

"Anastasia, I look forward to our date together. I will be in touch tomorrow."

He was already calling it a date. It would maybe make her feel less guilty to not think of it as a formal date but the situation would be unchanged. She had just given her number to another man and willingly agreed to be taken out on a date by him.

"Me too Brad," she replied. Even just saying his name for the first time elicited a shot of excitement in her.

At that moment the captain announced on the intercom that they were about to land and for all passengers and crew to be seated. She exchanged a last smile and glance with Brad as she made her way back to her cabin spot. The smiles from Lucy and Jessica that greeted her told the story. Anastasia strapped herself in for landing, there was turbulence in the air tonight. But maybe a lot more on the ground to come with Brad. Fasten your seatbelts...

Chapter Three

On her way home from Heathrow Anastasia was a cauldron of emotions. She had not told Lucy or Jessica that she had arranged a date with the gorgeous passenger. She did not want a barrage of questions and interrogation from them, and no doubt a touch of bitchy jealousy. But her main concern was of course Timothy. How would he react? Yes, he had suggested maybe her seeing another man if she wanted to, but was he actually serious about that? It was one thing for it to be a fantasy but quite another to become a reality. Yes, she loved Timothy, but the harsh reality was that sexually she did not feel fulfilled by him. She never had been.

It was not just the fact that physically he was not what she dreamt of, him being only 5'9 in height and not exactly well endowed in the trouser department. But also, he was working in a poorly paid job with no career prospects, while they were still living in a rented flat in a cheap part of the city.

She earned more than him as a flight attendant which as a modern woman shouldn't bother her, she thought, but deep down it did. Her friends such as Lucy and Jessica were always telling her privately that she could do better than him but so far, she had ignored them. Timothy was so sweet and good to her she thought, but could this go on forever? Maybe meeting someone else would add a much-needed spark to their relationship.

She had read an article in Vogue magazine recently where women had been with other men with the agreement of their partner, and it had worked wonders in the bedroom for the relationship. Could becoming a 'cuckold' and 'hot wife' be the catalyst to save their relationship? Brad had made an incredible impression on her in just one first encounter. Her black panties were still tingling with a touch of slight wetness from her excitement due to him from the flight.

She would mention to Timothy what he had previously suggested and what had happened on the flight tonight. But what she could not mention yet to him was just how excited she had been by Brad. Her wet panties on the ride home in the uber cab was evidence of that.

When Anastasia woke the next morning, the first thing she did was to check her phone for any messages from Brad. She was disappointed that so far there was nothing from him. She was already like some besotted teenager. He had been the last thing she had thought of before she went to sleep and now, he was the first thing she had thought of when she woke.

She looked over to the other side of the bed where Timothy was still asleep. At least he was not snoring again this time. His stomach showing signs of someone who regularly ate burgers and fries at his desk during lunchtime. However, today she didn't want to give him a hard time over any of his inadequacies because she wanted him in a good frame of mind. She was going to tell him about Brad.

"How was your flight last night Hun?" he asked her over breakfast.

"Oh, it was ok. The usual." It was the normal type of conversation Anastasia and Timothy would engage in after one of her flights. She would normally tell him about obnoxious passengers, ridiculous delays and hilarious stories from the crew.

However, the downside was more than compensated for by the glamorous locations she went to and chance to meet movie actors and rock stars as passengers. Timothy on the other hand most adventurous recent tale involved calling out a plumber to fix a broken toilet for some grandmother whose son was visiting for the weekend.

She did not want to hear similar today so she was going to take the plunge. "Timothy, you know what you mentioned the other night and maybe spicing things up between us?" He suddenly perked up from his slouch on the kitchen table and put down the newspaper he was reading.

"Yes of course, why?"

"Well, I've been thinking about what you said and maybe I'd like to try it. Just to see if it would, you know, add something to our relationship". She took a sip of her coffee in anticipation of his reaction. She need not have worried as a broad smile broke out on his face.

"That is great Hun, fantastic that you want to try it."

He was as surprised as he was excited that she had changed her mind and was now embracing a potential hot wife and cuck dynamic between them. "Was there erm, anyone you had in mind"? he asked with a trace of nervousness. There was a silence across the table for a few seconds.

"Yes, there is actually. He was a passenger on my flight last night. We got chatting, he seemed friendly, so we arranged to meet sometime perhaps. It will probably be for a quick drink and nothing more."

Anastasia hoped her attempt to downplay it would allay any fears Timothy had. He was a combination of excitement and nerves at hearing this coming from her. It was what he wanted and had suggested of course. But to hear her now reveal that she had taken up his idea, and already arranged a potential date with another man had shocked him. The bulge in his trousers told him it was the kind of shock he liked as he could feel his cock growing uncomfortably.

 Unfortunately, the bulge was not big enough in his trousers for her to notice.

"Who is he?" he quickly asked. Anastasia, feeling more relaxed now, felt able to divulge more information. "He is a businessman from the U.S, lives in New York and London, or Knightsbridge to be precise."

"Knightsbridge?" Timothy asked. "He must be rich."

"Maybe," Anastasia coyly replied. For the first time a half smile appeared on Anastasia's face. The exact same thought had of course already entered her mind. She did not want to dwell on it to avoid increasing any insecurity Timothy might be feeling.

 Suddenly her phone buzzed with a text message. She immediately saw the first line.

'Hi Anastasia, its Brad.' Instantly her heart was racing. She opened up the whole message.

'Hope you are on for a date tonight. I have booked us a table at The Ivy. Let me know your address and I will pick you up at 9pm. Brad.' She had not expected him to arrange things so fast, but maybe she should have known she told herself that a man like him does not stand on ceremony. She texted back immediately.

'Hi Brad! Yes, I would love to meet you tonight. I have never been to The Ivy, I can't wait! Anastasia xxxx' Were the four kisses too much too soon? She did not care. She sent her address just as Timothy came back into the kitchen.

"Who are you texting?" he asked.

"It's Brad. He is taking me to, I mean we are going to a restaurant.

Tonight."

"Oh, I see," Timothy expressed a degree of surprise. "Tonight? That is fast. Which restaurant?".

"It's The Ivy" she replied.

This was the restaurant that Timothy had been trying to get a table at for the past six months to try and impress Anastasia, but could not due to its exclusivity. Although he was secretly relieved that he had not been able to, as the menu was very expensive and beyond his means. How could this guy get a table there at such fast notice?

"You don't mind do you"? Anastasia asked him, "I will call it off if you want me to, but I think it could be exciting for us both."

 Her desire to do this was becoming more obvious to Timothy.

"I want you to do this, I don't mind at all. I hope you have a lovely evening with him". He was obviously still feeling aroused at the prospect of her going out with another man, but there were also nerves.

 "Thank you, Timothy, it's so good of you to allow this. Not many men would." She patted him on the shoulder in an appreciative manner. "He is picking me up at 9pm so I better get ready." Timothy could not fail to notice Anastasia's genuine excitement.

"Get ready for him you mean," he whispered to her.

Anastasia looked at him and smiled, "Yes for him". It was now out in the open, an idea which had previously seemed taboo was now about to be fulfilled. Anastasia was going out on a date with another man.

Anastasia looked through her wardrobe in the bedroom searching for the perfect outfit to wear tonight. She was searching through her outfits when her phone buzzed again. It was from Brad. Her heart raced again.

"What will you wear for me tonight, Hun?"

She was taken aback by the brashness, but she had to admit she kind of liked it. This made a contrast to the placid and gentle (too gentle?) ways of Timothy. She now wanted to please Brad and look good for him.

"What would you like me to wear for you Brad xxx?" she texted him. The answer came back immediately.

"I want you in a tight black dress, with heels, black lingerie and stockings seamed at the back." Wow. This was a man who knew exactly what he wanted and wasn't afraid to ask for it.

"Yes of course I will for you. Love Anastasia x". After sending she wondered if she had been too compliant with Brad. Should she have not done so for Timothy's sake? But it had been a long time since she had dressed up for a date.

In her wardrobe she pulled out her favourite dress, a black Versace number given to her when she modelled at London Fashion week last year. Perfect. She had not worn it since as there didn't seem much point when she was only going to pubs and cheap restaurants with Timothy.

She laid out her favourite set of lingerie on the bed. Victoria's Secret black bra(34b) and thong, with hold up stockings laid out on the bed ready to be worn. But not for Timothy. Tonight, it was for Brad. She spent longer in the shower than normal preparing herself, soaping herself all over with excessive lava. She was rightfully proud of her body. She did have the body of a supermodel with her breasts complimenting her slim frame, and her long legs smooth and glowing. She delicately trimmed her pussy in the shower. She didn't know if anything would happen with Brad tonight but it just felt right to do it. Just in case perhaps? Would Brad like her trimmed?

She had to stop asking herself these questions and get ready. Timothy had been nervously pacing up and down the bedroom while Anastasia was in the shower. The sight of her lingerie lying on the bed ready be worn, but for another man brought home the reality to him.

Anastasia came out of the shower wrapped in a white towel combing her long beautiful blonde hair whilst looking in the mirror. He had to sit on the bed and watch as she slowly put on the bra and panties. Her ass looked so tight and pert in the thong; her crack barely covered by it. The cheeks smooth and peachy. The sheer fabric was see through so there was just a tantalizing glimpse of the joy of her pussy. Her pink nipples protruding from under her bra. Then she slowly put on the stockings, and Timothy had to take a sharp intake of breath to stem his increasing exhilaration at this.

"You look amazing" he told her.

"Thank you" she quietly responded.

"He will think so too," Timothy remarked. She wanted to say "I hope so as well" but refrained.

The tight black Versace dress fitted her figure like a glove.

"Wow just wow," he proclaimed as she checked herself in the mirror and carefully applied her red lipstick and makeup.

She asked him to zip her dress up which he gleefully did.

"Are you sure he will like it?" she nervously asked, now seeking some form of reassurance.

"Oh my God yes, he would be crazy not to" Timothy assured her. "You look stunning". She was able to wear her high heels for tonight as she didn't have to worry about towering over the man as she did when wearing them with just 5'9 Timothy. Brad's 6'2 tall height allowed her this feminine luxury.

Timothy kissed her on the cheek. "I love you, Anastasia. Please let me know when you get to the restaurant and send me a pic." She was a bit surprised at this request but thought it could be fun.

"Of course, I will send pics, if you want me to."

"Yes, I really do," he enthusiastically told her. It would arouse him to see pictures of her at a restaurant with another man.

Then the doorbell rang. It was 9:00 pm. It was Brad, right on time just as he said he would be.

"'Its him!" Anastasia eagerly announced. She did some last-minute adjustments of her earrings and a final check of herself in the mirror. The scent of her sensual Chloe love story perfume floated in the bedroom. Timothy went over to kiss her goodbye but Anastasia was seemingly more concerned about picking up her handbag to leave and it resulted in a rather awkward peck on the cheek.

As she hurriedly made her way down the stairs Timothy could not fail to notice her tight ass and long legs wrapped in the tight dress. The sound of her high heels walking down the stairs echoed in the hallway. As she opened the door Anastasia held her breath.

"Hi! How are you?" she joyfully greeted him.

 "I am great Hun and you?" He was as handsome and tall as she had remembered on the flight. "Let's go Hun, you look beautiful and our table awaits".

 Timothy, who had been listening to every word at the top of

the stairs, was struck by the deep American voice and how authoritative and assured Brad sounded. He rushed into the bedroom by the window to catch a glimpse of them leaving. He was shocked by how tall and tanned Brad was, in an expensive navy-blue suit. Much better looking than what he had expected or what Anastasia had told him.

She was already giggling with him like a schoolgirl as he led her to his car, placing his hand on her back as he towered over her. He led her to a bright red Ferrari Spider car which made Timothy gulp. He drives a Ferrari?? He could see Anastasia's eyes light up when she saw it.

"Oh, wow this is yours!?" he heard her gush. "I've never been in a Ferrari".

 "Tonight, you are. Jump in," he replied as he opened the car door for her.

Timothy could spot Brad's eyes lingering on Anastasia's long legs as she got in the passenger seat. He was hoping that she might look up to him as she must have known that he would have been watching from the bedroom window. But she did not. She was already too engrossed in Brad.

The roar of the Ferrari engine filled the street as they sped away at fast speed. As he stood back from the window, Timothy had to sit down on the bed and take it all in. His heart was still pounding from the buzz of what he had just seen and his cock was rock hard.

 But there was unease too. When he had suggested this idea, he assumed that it would be with some regular guy just like him. He had not expected it to be with some Ferrari driving Adonis. The fact that he was obviously better looking and more successful than him made Timothy feel nervous. Still aroused yes but also restless and indeed inadequate. For the next couple of hours all he could do was wait by his phone for her texts. It was out of his hands. Anastasia was now in the hands of Brad.

Chapter Four

As they made their way to the restaurant Anastasia noticed the attention the car got from people as they dashed along. It felt so good to be the centre of attention.

"You look stunning Anastasia," he told her again. She was so happy to hear it from him.

"Exactly what I asked for," he remarked with satisfaction as he clapped eyes on the beautiful black dress and long stockinged legs.

"They are seamed at the back too Brad, just as you asked for".

"Yes, I noticed". He placed his left hand on her thigh while simultaneously holding the steering wheel with his right hand. She felt nice and silky he thought. Anastasia wondered if his hand would go further but he just left it there for a few enticing seconds. She did not make any attempt to stop him. It had felt too thrilling.

They had now arrived at the Ivy restaurant. As they entered the staff recognised Brad immediately. "Good evening, Mr Caulfield, so nice to see you again. Your usual table is ready for you."

He was evidently regular clientele of this restaurant. They had a perfect location by the window, overlooking a picturesque view of London at night. The sun was just going down on a summer night, creating a dark intimate spot in the corner just for them. How many other women had enjoyed this location with him she wondered? That thought didn't annoy her, if anything it made her feel special that she was one of the lucky ones. He was so self-assured when ordering for them both from the menu.

Over champagne and dinner, she discovered that Brad was a hedge fund manager in charge of the investment millions of his wealthy clients.

"Basically, I look after the money of the elites," he laughed. "It keeps a roof over my head".

"It certainly does" she teased him, "being able to drive a Ferrari and eat here regularly it must". She was always telling Timothy to start investing money into the stock market but he'd always told her he didn't have enough saved up and it was too complicated to understand.

She was enchanted by Brad's tales of high society in New York and London. He was spending the next month in London, and being a tennis fan was looking forward to Wimbledon. Naturally having centre court tickets for the men's final of course. He had been single for three months having split earlier in the year from his French model girlfriend Daniella. "She could not tame me" he laughed. "She wanted us to settle down together and I'm not quite ready for that yet". Anastasia had been listening intently.

"Maybe you need a woman who will not try to tame you, who will understand your need to live". The gaze between them lingered in the air. He held her hand under the table running his thumb over fingers.

The moment was broken by the sound of her phone vibrating with a text message.

"I'm sorry," she frustratingly murmured as she looked at her phone. Shit it was Timothy! She had been so captivated with Brad for the past hour in the restaurant that she had forgotten to text him when they had arrived as she was supposed to.

"Hi Hun is everything ok? Pls let me know xx". There were also two missed calls from him. She texted him back but couldn't hide her annoyance that it had interrupted the moment with Brad.

"Yes, everything is fine" was her curt response. She was about to put her phone in her handbag when the response came back immediately.

"Great. Thinking of you. Remember what I said earlier re sending me a pic. Thks. x". She thought this was slightly annoying but maybe she should send him one pic just to let him know she was okay.

Anastasia took the opportunity to tell Brad that she was involved with a man, but that he knew about her meeting him tonight. In fact, it was him who had thought of the idea first as a way of "hotting up" the relationship. Brad was not fazed by this at all and seemed to enjoy even more the prospect of being out on a date with another man's wife. It was far from the first time.

 He obliged by taking the pic as she held up a glass of champagne with a nice white smile against the backdrop of the window. Sent. 30 seconds later the response came back.

 "You look amazing, could you possibly send me one of you and him together?" She thought this could be perhaps a little bit awkward, but also exciting. Timothy had asked for it and if he did not like it, he could delete it couldn't he?

 "Brad, let's take a pic together by this window with the beautiful view," she flirtatiously asked him. He needed no encouragement.

 "Sure," he eagerly replied.

The waiter took the pic for them, Brad's arm around her waist as their heads touched together gently. "Smile" asked the waiter as he clicked on Anastasia's phone. She was positively beaming in her smile alongside Brad's cheeky grin, whilst exuding his masculine confidence and aura.

"A beautiful pic of you two," said the waiter as he handed the phone back to her. It certainly was. She was taken aback at how elated she looked standing next to Brad as he towered over her. They looked the perfect couple. It had been a long time since she had glowed in such a way with Tim in a pic with her eyes so sparkling and alive. She sent it to him expecting a quick response. This time however there was no immediate response. As Brad returned to their table and Anastasia went to the bathroom to fix her make up, there was still no response from Timothy to their pic. She was applying lipstick next to the large mirror in the luxurious restroom when her phone ping echoed. She knew it was him.

"You look so beautiful and happy. I wish I was there :("She was relieved that he was not angry, but could detect for the first time a touch of sadness from him.

She had no time to dwell on that if it was the case.

"Thks. I will be back later". She did not want to specify a time that she would return as that would put a limitation on her time with Brad. She then switched the phone off. She wanted no more distractions.

With an extra spring in her step, she walked back to the table, the sound of her heels against the marble floor made her legs seem even longer to Brad as he took the opportunity to gaze upon her as she made her way back. She had the catwalk model walk of course, and he had already seen it on display upon watching her walk up and down the aisle on the flight. Her full elegance was on display. On display just for him.

"Anastasia let's go. I will get the bill." He paid the bill on his card, leaving a hefty tip to the waiter as well.

"Thank you Brad I had a truly wonderful evening".

"It's not over yet Hun," he retorted.

"Oh Brad, is this your wild side coming out?" Slowly crossing and uncrossing her long legs deliberately her flirtatious manner was now unmistakable.

They thanked the waiter and front of house staff, and on reception they wished them a good night.

"Thank you, Mr Caulfield, hope to see you again Sir". Even in a restaurant full of high calibre clientele he was a valued member. Brad held her hand as they walked out of the restaurant. It was a hot night. And maybe about to get hotter.

Chapter Five

As they made their way towards Anastasia's place Brad's hand firmly remained on her thigh while driving. His skill in being able to drive simultaneously, one hand on the steering wheel and one hand on her thigh was so erotic to her. The excitement of the evening could no longer be contained. His warm hand began to feel under her dress to reveal her stocking tops.

"I wore them just for you. I don't even bother wearing them for Timothy these days," she told him in an almost hushed tone.

If it was wrong then why did it feel so good? Brad had a job keeping his eyes on the road as Anastasia went further and hoisted up her dress to reveal her black panties.

"And I wore these for you too, just as you asked for". Brad narrowly avoided hitting the car in front as Anastasia's knickers were on full display for him. Without hesitation he slid his finger under her knickers into her already wet pussy lips. She was glad she had trimmed herself earlier.

He was used to fully wet pussy but this one was already well lubricated considering he had barely touched her yet. He did not know what a dry pussy felt like, such was his effect on women. Anastasia laid back in the seat, placing her head against the head board. Closing her eyes, she could feel two fingers gently enter her. She let out a gentle moan, the type of moan she had not made in a long time. Brad was able to negotiate the road while skilfully teasing her pussy. Two fingers inside her then three. Her moistness increasing with each circular motion he made with his fingers. He could both feel and hear the wetness now, his glistening fingers evidence of her lust for him.

As they approached a set of traffic lights Brad told her to take down her undies. She dutifully manoeuvred herself in the tight space of the car seat and pulled them down, letting them fall to her heels and wrapped around her ankles.

Brad took the opportunity while stopped at the lights to lean over and kiss Anastasia passionately. His lips locked with hers, their tongues delicately exploring each other's mouth with such pent-up passion. She had never been kissed so passionately before. Never by Timothy. And never so skilfully. "'Oh Brad," she murmured as the lights turned green and the Ferrari sped on, "You're so fucking sexy". He had heard this many times from lots of women but he still loved hearing it.

Anastasia quickly moved herself to get closer to him and kissed his neck, nibbling away at his left ear as he somehow kept his eyes on the road. The masculine scent of his Givenchy Cologne aroused her further. Her hand rested on his left thigh, but it was now impossible to ignore the huge bulge in his trousers. It was asking to be let free and she was going to oblige. Anastasia felt the hardness and stiffness of it through the fabric of his trousers, her hand caressing it to the sound of Brads gentle moans.

She could feel he was BIG. Anastasia had never experienced a truly big cock before and had always wanted to at least once in her life. Friends like Lucy and Jessica were always telling her the joys of being with a man with a big cock. And the harsh reality was that was never going to happen with Timothy.

"Brad, I want to suck you so much. Please let me suck your cock!". She surprised herself with how direct she was.

"Let me pull over Hun, I know a quiet spot just here". He knew exactly where to go.

The car pulled over to a quiet off road, on a parking location of an office complex. Fortunately, at 11.30pm on a Saturday night it was deserted. The Ferrari had barely stopped when Anastasia already began to unbuckle his trouser belt. They kissed passionately again, her pulling down his trousers as he raised himself from the seat, while she impatiently yanked down his trousers and white CK boxers. Then she saw it. OMFG. It was HUGE.

"Oh my God you are so big! Wow!!".

Anastasia gasped with lustful joy and anticipation. The tip of it was already glistening and shining, its thickness impressed her as well as the incredible length. It must be a full 9" inches she guessed as it sprang up so firmly and proud. Timothy was only around 3" when soft and not erect. Brad was now 3 times the size. 3 times the man Timothy is she reflected. Brad loved the excitement and expression on women's faces when they saw it for the first time.

"Have a feel Anastasia," he commanded her as he settled back in his reclining seat.

"Oh, fuck yes I will," she purred as she eagerly grasped it, thinking it felt as hard as a rock as she held the base.

Even his pubic hair was perfect, just the right amount on his magnificent balls she judged. She wanted to examine, explore and saviour it. The tip of it was fully engorged, the blue vein ran the whole seemingly endless length of it. It was like a skyscraper building that soared above a city.

Anastasia was almost in a trance.

"Suck it for me Hun," he instructed. She needed no encouragement as her head moved down towards his lap. She wondered if the size would be too much for her mouth, but Brad guided it gently into the warmth of her mouth. He wanted the deep throat that he was accustomed to from his women. The large tip hit the back of her welcoming mouth as he increased the pace, pulling her head down faster to increase the rhythm. His penis felt gigantic inside her mouth as he pulled the dress down her shoulders exposing her black bra to him for the first time. He expertly unhooked her bra, throwing it to the car floor as the sight of her erect pink nipples greeted him. All the time she was continuing to suck him deeply.

"More baby more," he whispered.

Anastasia's mouth was being severely contorted by the severe drilling it was getting. Her cheeks becoming puffed out as he pushed his dick in and out. Saliva was beginning to dribble onto her chin and fall on the seat.

She used her tongue to lick up and down the full length from the base to tip, and down again. Lipstick marks were visible all over the shaft now. Brad could feel his tip smack against her tonsils and back of her throat. No one had ever been this deep in her mouth before, they had neither been capable or physically well-endowed enough. She was in reality a mouth fuck virgin before now but Brad was changing that tonight.

"Fuck you suck so good!" he groaned.

Anastasia felt she was about to gag and instinctively he allowed her head up in order for her to breathe. Gasping for an intake of air, her mouth was temporarily freed from his control. Her saliva and his precum had mixed in her mouth and fallen from her lips to form a small puddle on the edge of the seat. His now shiny cock seemed to be even harder and stronger, as she looked down at how her mouth and lips had encased it with her saliva and lipstick.

Anastasia's lipstick and make up was not only smudged on his shirt and neck, but also on his magnificent dick. He took her head in his hands, kissing her again with wild passion.

"Come here," he beckoned her, opening the car door and getting out, temporarily pulling his trousers up. She took his hand and climbed over the gearbox, kicking off her heels so she slid over the front seats and followed him out on his side. She did not bother to adjust her torn off dress, exposing her breasts and pussy.

Brad hoisted her up as she got out, her arms around his neck whilst he carried her to the front of the car. It was like a groom carrying his bride over the threshold she thought. But he was not carrying a bride to get married, he was carrying her to the bonnet of his Ferrari to fuck her senseless. Anastasia had barely noticed the night stars on this warm summer night, the stars were shining not just in the sky but also in her head.

The car lights being still on illuminated the scene. He gently laid her down on the bonnet, her arms still around his neck, she knew she could trust him to hold her tight as he did. Brad unbuttoned his shirt and Anastasia finally got to see his beautiful, tanned and toned physique. The lights enhanced his strong arms, broad shoulders, defined pecs and chiselled six pack. She instinctively reached out to feel his chest with her hands, her fingers tracing the contours of his pecs and stomach. How smooth and glowing he felt compared to Timothy's rather hairy and pasty body. His hours in the gym with a personal trainer had clearly paid off.

She manoeuvred herself under him as Brad slowly teased her moist vaginal lips with his enormous tip. He was tantalizing her as she felt it slide along her opening, gently probing with the head. The pussy lips being prised open bit by bit but not yet fully penetrated by this huge weapon.

"Please Brad, I need you inside me! Fuck me now I want it so fucking much!" She was almost begging him in lustful desperation.

But he knew how to tease and wait for the perfect moment. He moaned as he entered her slowly at first, knowing her pussy would feel tight. All pussys were tight to a man of his size, but he knew he had the skill and expertise to ease himself inside. His first thrust shook Anastasia to the core. He instantly felt the wetness and heat. Even by the standards of the countless wet pussys he had been in, this was a soaking wet one. Her moistness welcomed him in, the wetness making his penetration easy despite the tightness and his rock hard 9 inches.

Anastasia was almost screaming now, thankful that no one was around to hear. Not that she would have cared if they did.

"FUCK ME BRAD, FUCK ME HARD!" she screamed. Her ass slid up and down the bonnet in tandem with his powerful thrusts. Her stockinged legs up in the air she rested them on his firm shoulders, giving him the angle to go even deeper inside her. She was being penetrated deeper than she had ever known before, Timothy could only dream of going so deep she thought.

This is how a real man fucks she kept thinking. She had denied herself pure sexual pleasure from a real man for too long. This was the fuck of her life: of anyone's life. The comparison between Brads powerful masculinity versus Timothy's lack of it was striking. It was cruel to Timothy and maybe her emotions were in lustful turmoil during this orgasmic heaven from Brad, but right now she could not control herself. She did not want the image of Timothy to ruin this intimate, special and outrageous moment with Brad.

"Fuck! Fuck! Fuck! You're such a real man! Yes!Yes!Yes!" She screamed.

The car seemed to be shaking as he pumped away. The sight of this beautiful and leggy blonde with her legs wrapped on his shoulders stretched out on the bonnet of his Ferrari, and begging to be fucked by him, was bringing Brad to the tipping point.

"Babe I'm gonna cum," he moaned in ecstasy as he sensed his balls growing heavy. Anastasia could also sense he was ready to cum, as her vagina was about to overflow and flood her entire body with orgasmic ecstasy.

Within seconds she felt the walls of her womb hit by a jet of seaman, it's warmth and power unmistakeable. His groans of pleasure were in sync with each spurt inside her. His brain turning orange in a sexual psychedelic high. Anastasia's body now convulsed in spasms as she orgasmed alongside him; her first orgasm in years. Her sexual frustration finally being released.

"Shoot your spunk right up me!" she begged. His ejaculation kept coming inside her as she gripped him tightly around the waist, pumping his potent seed deep inside her.

Each shot of spunk he sprayed up her was a dagger for the respect of Timothy. Brad quickly pulled his cock out and let her slide off the bonnet to crouch down on her knees to take the final glorious spurts in her mouth. One shot, two shot and finally a third shot into her gaping welcoming mouth as she closed her eyes. Her tongue swirling the creamy liquid she had been given from one side of her mouth to the other.

"You taste so good," swallowing it all slowly she moaned.

He tasted much better than Timothy who unfortunately seemed to have a rather sour taste, but Brad's sperm was sweet and succulent. He let out a final groan of sexual bliss, having to rest against the car to compose himself. They were both finally spent, and needed a collective sharp intake of breath after what had just happened. There was a puddle of seaman and saliva on the ground, and Anastasia's lips and cheeks were covered in spunk. It had sprayed onto her dress and stockings too.

She did not know it was possible for a man to ejaculate so much. His cum was much more voluminous, thick and creamy than Timothy's tiny watery drops she reflected.

"You are amazing Brad," she declared looking up at him as she licked the last drops from his tip, holding it in her right hand still crouched down. It was still remarkably firm and enormous considering it had just ejaculated a huge amount.

She wanted to hold it all night if she could.

"Anastasia you are wild!" he laughed. They both giggled and adjusted their clothes, Brad helping her up from her knees and giving her a pat on her ass as she tiptoed her way back into the car. Her knickers were still on the seat with the high heels on the floor on her passenger side. She wiggled them on again noticing that her still soaking vagina dampened the fabric and leaving a visible wet spot.

Brad buttoned up his shirt and trousers, "How do you feel now?" he asked.

"I feel incredible, and very naughty thanks to you," she giggled. Anastasia used the mirror to fix her now dishevelled hair and apply some lipstick. Some tissues from the dashboard were needed to wipe away the fresh seaman on her face and dry the obvious stains on her dress and stockings. With his cum still inside her and his cologne on her it would not be possible to wipe away everything. Brad had left too much of his mark on her for that, both physical and emotional.

Chapter Six

The engine roared as the car drove away and back towards her home. The streets were almost empty at this hour apart from the late-night revellers walking home and couples' arm in arm. Anastasia pondered that none of them would match the mind-blowing sex she and Brad had enjoyed tonight. She thought she better switch on her phone and let Timothy know she was on her way; it had been over two hours since she had switched it off. It vibrated instantly with WhatsApp notifications.

'Tim: 2 missed calls: 1 new message: Hi Hun when r u coming back? Thought u would be back by now luv u Tim xx'

It was a reminder of the reality she was now facing. Timothy had encouraged this and was excited by it, but had he bargained for what he was actually letting himself in for? He had under estimated the effect of encouraging his woman to spend time with another man like Brad. A man like Brad who was dangerous to the husbands and boyfriends of the women he met. And seduced.

"Is that little Timmy?" he asked mockingly.

"Yes, I'm afraid so," she chuckled making no attempt to defend her husband. She did not feel the need to respond back as she would be home in 10 minutes anyway. Brad was going to Paris the following weekend and invited Anastasia for dinner at the Ritz, a favourite spot of his in Paris. She was supposed to be going around Timothy's parents for a boring Sunday dinner that same weekend, but there was no way now she was going to turn down a weekend in Paris with Brad. Timothy would have to find some excuse to cancel with his parents.

In stark terms she would rather be Brad's whore than Timothy's wife right now.

"I want to spend more time with you, a better man, a superior man," she declared. "I wanted you the minute I saw you on the plane". She immediately realised the implications of what she had just said but it felt natural and indeed good to say it.

 Her relationship with Timothy could never be the same. Hopefully he could accept and indeed enjoy her new and exciting passionate relationship with her new Adonis lover. This was an opportunity for his cuck fantasies to be fulfilled. Brad had shown Anastasia in just one night what real sex, real passion and indeed what a real man is.

The car approached her house and she could see the lights were still on. Timothy was still up and had not gone to bed, still waiting for her. Would she tell him tonight everything that had happened? A new exciting chapter in her life as a hot wife had just begun. She was not just going to embrace it. She was going to be fucked senseless by it.

THE END

About The Author

Tj Mack

TJ Mack lives in London, UK. He wants to bring real emotion to erotic literature. When not writing he can be found listening to rock music and enjoying new cuisine.
Contact for queries and projects at
tjmacknow@gmail.com
Insta:tj_mack_author

www.ingramcontent.com/pod-product-compliance
Lightning Source LLC
Chambersburg PA
CBHW051936150726
47999CB00006B/2242